JACK SPLAT

Superfly Pest

With thanks to Hannah Cornish and Nigel Wyatt from the Natural History Museum for their help with fly facts. To Sophie McKenzie and Claire Wilson for letting me be a pest! Also, to my nephew Henry, from your Ant ~ LK

To my little pest, Alice ~ AR

STRIPES PUBLISHING
An imprint of Magi Publications
1 The Coda Centre, 189 Munster Road, London SW6 6AW

A paperback original
First published in Great Britain in 2011

Text copyright © Lou Kuenzler, 2011
Illustrations copyright © Andrew Rowland, 2011

ISBN: 978-1-84715-142-1

The right of Lou Kuenzler and Andrew Rowland to be identified as the authors and illustrator of this work respectively has been asserted by them in accordance with the Copyright, Designs and Patents Act, 1988.

A CIP catalogue record for this book is available from the British Library.

Printed and bound in the UK.

2 4 6 8 10 9 7 5 3 1

JACK SPLAT

Superfly Pest

Lou Kuenzler

Illustrated by Andrew Rowland

Stripes

Hello up there!

Yes, you, Buddy. You with the two legs, reading this book.

Can you see me? Here I am! Down here.

Handsome, aren't I?

I'm Jack ... Jack Splat – hero of this story!

Let's get one thing straight, right from the start, Buddy-Two-Legs. Do NOT slam the book and try to squash me...

I said, do NOT slam the book!

SPLAT!

Well, that's the end of the story.
SPLAT! I'm dead. SPLAT! You killed me.
SPLAT! This is the ghost of Jack Splat
talking to you. Because you killed me, I
am going to haunt you FOR EVER.

Buzz! Whoooo!

Buzz! Whoooo!

Just kidding.

Here I am!

It takes more
than a book to kill me.

I think that might have been my
thirty-third cousin Connor that you
just squelched, though. Shame. He was
a nice guy (or nice fly, should I say?).

JACK SPLAT

Anyway, this isn't Connor's story
(which is lucky, otherwise you'd be
saying "That was a RUBBISH book!").
This is MY story – Jack Splat! And no
one can SPLAT me. I am a supersonic,
super-duper, super-fantastic fly.

I'm eight days old today!

♫ *Happy birthday to me!* ♫ ♪
Drink a pool of cat wee. ♫
And because it's my birthday,
♪ *Eat a dog poo for free!*

Eight days ago,
I hatched out of my
egg – POP!
I was nothing
more than a tiny,
wiggly maggot.

Even as a baby
I was handsome.
Don't you agree?

Jack, aged 1 hour

JACK SPLAT

The dustbin where I was born was full of BRILLIANT things to eat.

On Monday I ate through one rotten tomato.

But I was still hungry.

On Tuesday I ate through two slimy bananas.

But I was still hungry.

On Wednesday I ate... (You might have heard this story before – or something like it. I'm sure you get the picture. I slurped and burped and ate some truly awesome stuff. But I WAS STILL HUNGRY!)

JACK SPLAT

So... On Saturday, I ate through one soggy nappy, one shrivelled verruca, one snotty tissue, one dead mouse, one hairy sausage and one pellet of hamster poo.

That night I had a stomach ache. But I wasn't hungry any more – and I wasn't a tiny maggot any more, either. I was a big fat juicy one!

I built a cosy pupa around myself and stayed inside for two days. Then I pushed my way out and ... (Wait for it...)

JACK SPLAT

I was a beautiful, buzzing housefly!

"Look at me! I'm not a wiggly
maggot any more," I cried, as I flapped
my wings and flew upside down round
the inside of an empty crisp packet.
Then I looped-the-loop through the
middle of a loo roll.

"Look, Mum!" I called. "I can fly!"

"Very nice," said Mum. But she
wasn't really watching. She was

busy laying 75 new eggs in a can of
old dog food.

"I'm all grown up," I said, hovering
in the air above her. "I'm a proper
flying fly!"

"Then you can act like a proper fly,"
said Mum, "and BUZZ OFF! It's time
to find somewhere of your own to live!
Go on! Shoo!"

JACK SPLAT

I'd be lying if I said that didn't hurt. I thought I was Mum's favourite. I thought of all her two thousand babies she could see that I was the special one. Turns out, she couldn't even remember my name.

"Goodbye, Alfie. Good luck."

"I'm not Alfie, Mum! I'm—"

"Bertie?"

"No, Mum!"

"Colin?"

"Nope."

"Dave?"

"NO!"

I left her guessing and buzzed sadly away towards the top of the bin.

"Eddie? Freddie? Gary? Harry?"

"No, no, no and no."

"Ian? J—"

JACK SPLAT

At that moment, a warm, sugary smell wafted past me on the breeze. YUM! The dustbin was full of gorgeous, rotten pongs. But nothing had ever smelt this SWEET!

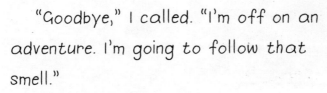

"Goodbye," I called. "I'm off on an adventure. I'm going to follow that smell."

Far below me, Mum's voice echoed round the deep, dark bin.

"Goodbye... Kenny? Lenny? Milo? Nigel?"

I was on my own now. A lone fly about to explore the BIG wide world and follow in the wing-flaps of famous flies before me.

FAMOUS FLIES

Christopher Columbuzz
Fly who discovered the New World

Swat of the Antarctic
Fly Polar Explorer

Neil Flewstrong
First Fly on the Moon

Buzz Allgone
Second Fly on the Moon

Splat Cousteau
Underwater Fly Explorer

One day, MY name would be on a Famous Fly poster, too! Jack Splat – Famous Explorer! I was destined for great adventures and daring deeds in the search for fly-tastic snacks.

No one (not even Mum) would forget my name ever again.

Chapter Two
Window Pain!

With a flap of my wings I was off – flying through the sky on my first real adventure. I followed the sweet smell on the wind, heading straight for the house beside our dustbin.

"Woo hoo!" I cried. "Nothing can stop me now! I'm Jack Spla—"

WHAM! OUCH!

OK, nothing except a window could stop me. I never even saw it coming! I landed *SPLAT* on the glass with my antennae all crumpled up.

JACK SPLAT

My Uncle Humph had warned me about windows back in the bin. "Tricky things," he'd said. "There doesn't seem to be anything there, but there is. Something...? Nothing...? It can drive a fly mad." Windows had certainly driven Uncle Humph mad. He was as nutty as a squirrel poo.

"But I'm young, clever and unsplattable!" I told myself. "A simple window can't defeat a fearless fly like me."

I took off from the windowsill, lined myself up and flew forward again — head down, wings low, flapping at top speed.

Perhaps, if I flew fast enough, the force of my super-strength would crack the window.

JACK SPLAT

"I *can* defeat the window! I *can* defeat the window! I *can* defeat the—"

WHAM! OUCH!

OK, I can't defeat the window.

I bounced off the glass and landed SPLAT on the windowsill again, in the six-legged splits!

JACK SPLAT

My head was buzzing – really buzzing, not just in the usual fly "buzzing about" sort of way. I pressed my eyes against the glass and tried to focus. (Normally, my super vision means every image I see is repeated eight thousand times in a single glance. But now, all I was getting was eight thousand different blurs.)

As I focused my eyes and stared in through the window, I spotted it... A **CAKE**! A beautiful chocolate **CAKE** sitting in the middle of the kitchen table.

JACK SPLAT

"Of course," I drooled. "That's where the sugary smell is coming from." And this wasn't a stale, dry cake like the kind we'd had back in the bin. This **CAKE** smelt sweet and freshly baked!

"I have to get inside that kitchen!" I cried. All I needed was a plan... A plan and a quick snack. Luckily, there was a streak of runny pigeon poo dripping down the windowpane. I paddled into the middle and slurped. The poo had a lovely, tangy cherry-berry flavour. So that was one of my five-a-day sorted.

JACK SPLAT

Thinking of a plan to get through
the window was a little more difficult.
Here's what I came up with:

> Plan 1: Break the glass with
> a fly-size hammer.

Good plan. But no hammer.

> Plan 2: Hope that an army of
> ants (like the ones who nest
> under our dustbin) come along
> and help me lift the window.

Good plan. But no an—
You are NOT going to believe this!
Just at that moment, a strange
noise rose above the buzzing in my
head. It sounded like drumming ... or the
march of tiny feet.

JACK SPLAT

Left! Right! Left! Right!
Forward march!

You've guessed it. Ants! Right on cue, a column of the busy little creatures came marching my way.

"Can you help me open this window?" I called.

Ants are really strong. Not that you'd think it to look at them, with their wobbly necks and weedy little waists like someone has tied an elastic band round their middles.

The ants ignored me.

"Wow, guys!" I cried cheerily. "That really is a straight line you're marching in. Any chance you could stop and lend me a leg?"

JACK SPLAT

The ants didn't even pause. They advanced on up the wall, singing a marching song in time to the sound of their feet.

Mind out, fly, we're coming through,
And we will march all over you.
We smell cake and we want some.
We will carry it, crumb by crumb!

"Wait!" I said. "That's my **CAKE**! I just wanted a bit of help to reach it, that's all."

The ants marched on past me.

You are a very stupid fly!
An empty-headed kind of guy!
If you detect a gorgeous pong,
Look for the gap it's coming from!

JACK SPLAT

"Gap?" I said. "What gap?"

I looked up and saw that the window was open a tiny crack at the very top. Of course! That's how the smell was drifting into the garden. Typical of ants to be so know-it-all and bossy about it, though. The ant leading the troop was the bossiest of them all. He must have been the Lieuten-ANT! As he set off up the wall, the others followed like horseflies after pony poo.

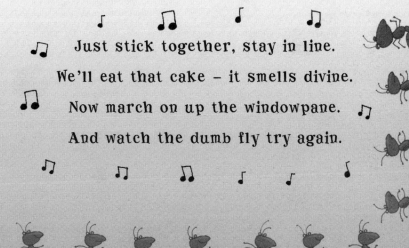

Just stick together, stay in line.
We'll eat that cake – it smells divine.
Now march on up the windowpane.
And watch the dumb fly try again.

Dumb fly? Who were they calling dumb?

I flapped to the top of the window.

"I knew about that gap all along," I said, buzzing over the ants' heads to take a closer look. "I'm an explorer! Flying through that gap was always part of my plan."

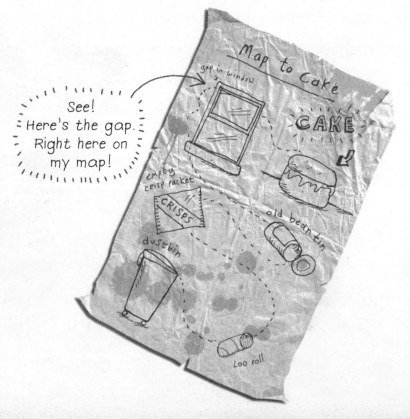

See! Here's the gap. Right here on my map!

Map to Cake

gap in window

CAKE

empty crisp packet

CRISPS

old bean tin

dustbin

Loo roll

Chapter Three
Mixing It Up!

Ants may have strength and brains and all that stuff, but what they really need is wings! They were still marching up the outside of the glass when – with one quick buzzzzzzzzzz – I flew through the gap in the window and into the kitchen.

"Bye, bye marching midgets," I called. "I'm off to eat **CAKE**!"

The **CAKE** smelt deliciously chocolatey – and it was all mine! I flicked my antennae, taking in the rich, sweet smell as I circled above it.

JACK SPLAT

"Here I come!" I swooped down on to the kitchen table and rubbed my front legs together in anticipation.

But just then, I felt a gust of wind. The kitchen door swung open and a human woman plodded into the room. "Great!" I groaned. "That's *all* I need! First windows, now humans."

This one certainly looked pretty dangerous. One swat from those HUGE hands and it would be *SPLAT* – bye bye, Jack. She smelt horribly flowery – like the pukey-perfumey whiff of roses you normally only find round a bee's bum.

I froze on the spot. "What now?"

The woman slurped from a mug of coffee as a smaller human appeared in the doorway.

JACK SPLAT

"Is that the cake for my birthday tea, Mum?"

Although he was only half the size of his mum, he still looked enormous to me! He was wearing really strange clothes – a cloak and tights, with his pants over the top! (I've got to tell you, that is NOT a good look!)

JACK SPLAT

"Yes, but don't touch, Ben!" said the woman, as he loomed over the CAKE. "There's not much time before your friends arrive." She plonked her mug of coffee on the table, a splash of scalding liquid narrowly missing me.

YIKES! I buzzed out of the way, and that was when she spotted me.

"A nasty fly!" she screeched, flapping her arms about. "Quick, Ben! Open the window so it can get out."

Great! *Now* she opens the window properly. If only she'd done that earlier, I'd be up to my knees in CAKE already. One thing was certain, though. I wasn't flying back out. Not without plunging my face into some of that CAKE first!

I shot up to the ceiling and hung upside down from the light. There was no way Mrs Flappy-Arms could get to me there. Clinging on by my super-sucky feet, I scanned the room, planning my best route back to the **CAKE**.

"Superboy to the rescue!" bellowed the kid, as he lolloped over to the window with his head down and his arms outstretched. (I think he was pretending to fly.) He skidded to a halt and stuck his finger up his nose.

"Huh! Call yourself Superboy – more like *Bogeyboy!*" I cried ... although of course he couldn't hear me.

He licked the tasty-looking snot off his finger and climbed up on to a stool to open the window.

Just then, I spotted that the Lieuten-ANT and his army were inside now, marching across the kitchen counter and into the fruit bowl.

Good, I thought. *Let them eat fruit. The* **CAKE** *is MINE!*

Bogeyboy thundered back to the table. "Thanks, Ben," said Mrs Flappy-Arms. "You really *are* a superhero!"

Him? A superhero? Is that what the silly pants were about? If he wanted to look like a superhero, he should have dressed up as ME!

JACK SPLAT – SUPERFLY!

1. Wings – These beat 200 to 300 times a second at an average speed of 4.5 miles per hour. OK, so it would take me quite a long time to get from London to Paris (47½ hours, actually) but, in most houses, I can do loo seat to lunch plate in about 36 seconds flat.

2. Eyes – My pair of bulging eyes is actually thousands of smaller eyes, which I use to see to the left, to the right, in front and above me – none of that ridiculous head turning you lot have to do.

3. Antennae – I smell with these: lovely smells like poo, rotting meat and CAKE.

4. Abdomen – What goes in must come out. It comes out quite a lot, actually; I poop every four to five minutes.

5. Proboscis – My mouth is like a long straw, so if food is liquid, I just slurp it straight up. But I don't have teeth to bite or chew, so if it is solid, I vomit up saliva and stomach juices until I make a nice slushy mush.

6. Hairy legs – These six beauties are used to taste everything I land on. That's right! I can decide what I want to eat just by standing on it. I'd like to see you choose a pizza with your toes!

7. Feet – These suckers can stick anywhere. Thanks to them, I can walk on windows, walls and even ceilings!

JACK SPLAT

Now that's what I call a superhero! But Mrs Flappy-Arms didn't seem to be a fly fan. I was buzzing round the light bulb, trying not to burn my bum, when she reached inside a drawer, brought out some shiny silver stuff and – wait for it – covered up the **CAKE**!

"That revolting little pest's still here," she said. "I can hear it buzzing about! Better be on the safe side."

She looked up at the light, but I was already on the other side of the room. With super-accurate aim, I swooped low and pooped in her coffee mug.

"That'll *teach* you to call me revolting!" I sniggered.

Then I hid in a plant on the windowsill.

"I can't hear it any more," said Mrs Flappy-Arms. "Hopefully it's gone." She then took a big gulp of coffee (and poo). "Mmmm." She

smiled. "Lovely! Now, I'd better get on and ice that cake, or it won't be ready for the party."

"Can we decorate it like an Egyptian mummy cake?" begged Bogeyboy. "With bandages, blood and gouged-out eyes!"

I had to admit, he might dress funny, but when it came to food this boy had taste!

"No," said Mrs Flappy-Arms firmly. "But I am going to make extra-gooey chocolate buttercream icing."

"Yum!" said Bogeyboy.

Again, I had to agree. Obviously, blood and eyeballs would improve even the finest CAKE, but extra-gooey icing sounded like a start.

I watched as Mrs Flappy-Arms put the ingredients into a bowl one by one. Then she turned to get something out of a drawer.

This was my chance!

I zipped over to the bowl and landed on top of a blob of butter.

I was about to plunge in my long proboscis when... YIKES! Mrs Flappy-Arms loomed over the bowl with something in her hand.

JACK SPLAT

Before I could escape, she began to beat everything – including me – around the bowl with a wooden spoon!

"Please stop ... please stop ... please stop!" I yelped, as I tumbled around the bowl.

JACK SPLAT

At last, the swirling *did* stop. PHEW!

My head still spinning, I tried to swim to the side, but the mixture was too thick. It was like a cow pat now – dark and brown and gloopy. It would have been chocolate heaven, had I not been so totally stuck.

"Help! Get me out!" I cried.

But it was hopeless. Mrs Flappy-Arms

removed the shiny stuff from the
CAKE, and spooned the chocolate
mixture – and ME – on to the top.
If Mrs Flappy-Arms had looked down,
she'd have seen me for sure, but,
luckily, Bogeyboy was busy with his
finger up his nose again.

"Stop that, Ben," she said. "It's
disgusting!"

JACK SPLAT

Disgusting? It looked delicious! Go for it, kid! If flies had noses, I know I'd pick mine all the time.

Bogeyboy stopped picking. But as soon as his mum turned her back, he sneaked up and stuck his finger – THE SAME FINGER – deep into the icing on top of the **CAKE**. I was starting to admire this kid. Snot and choc – that's got to taste good, right?

Uh-oh!

The only trouble was, when he lifted his finger to lick it, there I was stuck on the end, knee-deep in extra-gooey icing.

Chapter Four
Horribly Clean!

"Please don't eat me! Please don't eat me!" I cried, struggling to get free. But there was no escape – Bogeyboy was going to swallow me whole!

Then, just as he lifted his finger to his lips, he spotted me.

"Cool!" he said. "I can see this fly's buggy eyes." He held me so close, I could see his big watery eyes reflected back at me eight thousand times. Gross!

"Look, Mum."

"Get rid of that thing, right NOW!" cried Mrs Flappy-Arms. "I bet it's been on the cake." She shuddered. "Flies are covered in thousands of germs!"

Millions, actually! I'm proud of my germs and I was scoring pretty high that day. I had, after all, come straight from the dustbin and snacked on pigeon poo on the way.

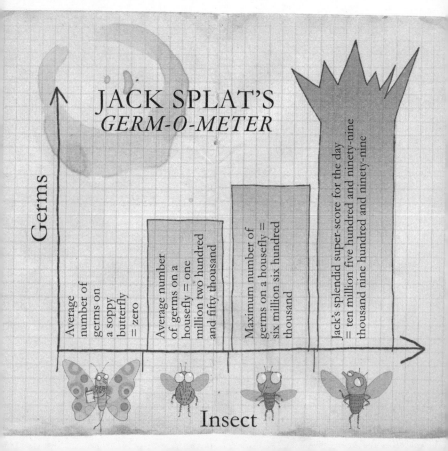

JACK SPLAT'S
GERM-O-METER

Germs

Average number of germs on a soppy butterfly = zero

Average number of germs on a housefly = one million two hundred and fifty thousand

Maximum number of germs on a housefly = six million six hundred thousand

Jack's splendid super-score for the day = ten million five hundred and ninety-nine thousand nine hundred and ninety-nine

Insect

JACK SPLAT

Not bad, eh?

Mrs Flappy-Arms dragged Bogeyboy to the sink. "Let's wash your hands and get rid of that fly!"

Now I've always wanted to explore the sewers. But if I had to be rinsed down the sink and plunged along the pipes first, I'd be soggy and dead by the time I got there.

I heard the rush of water as she turned on the tap. I had to get out of there – fast. But I was covered in icing and Bogeyboy was holding me with one wing pinched between his huge sausagey fingers. If I so much as trembled, my wing would be snapped off. What I needed was an emergency plan...

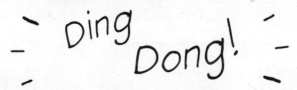

Ding Dong!

What I got was a doorbell.

"That must be the first of your friends," said Mrs Flappy-Arms.

She grabbed a soggy dishcloth from the sink and before I knew it, everything went dark. I found myself bumped and shaken as she scrubbed the icing from Bogeyboy's hands.

"Argh! Careful! Mind what you're doing!" I yelped.

I heard her muffled voice. "Go and let your friend in, Ben." Then thump ... thump ... thump as Bogeyboy clomped out of the room. Next, I felt myself fall through the air as Mrs Flappy-Arms threw the cloth down in the sink. By the time I'd struggled through the soggy folds, the last of the icing had been washed off my legs. There was

JACK SPLAT

nothing left but the bitter, lemon-
fresh taste of washing-up liquid.
YUCK!

I crawled out of the sink and up on
to the draining board. "Stop!" I cried,
as I helplessly watched Mrs Flappy-
Arms put the **CAKE** in the fridge and
shove the icing bowl in
the dishwasher. Then
she squirted EVERYTHING
with a yucky, spluttery,
hideously fresh and
lemony, super-clean, 100%
germ-killing, wipey, washy
spray. I couldn't believe
it! There wasn't a
smudge of icing or a
crumb of **CAKE** left
anywhere!

Hideously fresh
and lemony,
super-clean,
100%
germ-killing,
wipey,
washy spray

Even the ants, who'd crawled out of the fruit bowl by now, couldn't find a crumb to eat.

"Forward march!" ordered the Lieuten-ANT.

There's just no point in staying here.
It's too clean now, that is quite clear.
But we know we are in the mood
To go and munch some party food!

"Party food?" I said, staggering across the draining board. "What party food?" My near-death experience had made me hungrier than ever.

The ants carried on with their silly, smug song.

JACK SPLAT

We sent a spy to have a look.
To check out what Ben's mum would cook.
There's crisps, pizza and jelly, too.
It's in the lounge, so let's march through!

"Oh! *That* party food," I said.
"I knew about *that* all along!"

"Liar!" said the last ant in line. She
was the smallest of them all – no
bigger than one of my super-sucky
feet. "You didn't even
know there would be
party food!" she
squeaked.

Liar!

"What?" I said. "I *cAN'T* hear you properly." Ants have tiny, squeaky little voices. That's why they march around in big armies singing together at top volume. It's the only way they can be heard.

But I am Jack Splat, the great explorer! If there was party food, I'd find it long before the pesky parade of ants. Bogeyboy had said the **CAKE** was for his birthday tea, so his mum would probably bring it through later. It all made sense now! It was clear that the lounge was the place I needed to be!

"You should get yourselves some pants, ants!" I laughed. "But you still wouldn't be as super as me!" And off I flew.

Chapter five
Fancy Pest Party

As soon as I was out of the kitchen,
I flicked my antennae, hoping for the
scent of party food. Nothing. But what
I *did* smell was the downstairs loo. As I
was already way ahead of the ants,
I squeezed through the gap at the top
of the door and popped in for a quick
drink – something to get rid of the
disgusting taste of the washing-up
cloth. The toilet water had a horrible
pine-fresh tang. But then I smelt out a
lovely grubby spot under the rim and
had a good slurp around there.

"A quick poop on the hand towel, and I'm done." I grinned. I'd still reach the party food long before the ants. But strangely I just couldn't smell it. Usually my super-sensitive antennae get a whiff of even the smallest crumb. Perhaps those marching midgets had been trying to trick me. As I came closer to the lounge, all I could smell was a mix of sweat, farts and cheesy feet.

The cause of the pong was obvious. The room was full of boys. They were getting sweatier by the minute – shouting and pushing, jumping up and down on the sofa, while Bogeyboy ripped the paper off a pile of presents. The guests were all wearing capes and tights with their pants on over the top, too!

JACK SPLAT

One huge kid had painted his face green. The colour reminded me of a lovely piece of rotting meat I'd seen in the dustbin one time. Another had a spider's web printed on his suit. (I admit that was pretty scary!) "But why didn't anyone dress up as a super-cool fly?" I wondered.

JACK SPLAT

"It must be here somewhere," I muttered, as I set off for a spot of on-the-ceiling surveillance, determined to discover where the party food was hiding.

There it was! Spread out on a long table at the back of the room was the party feast. There were sandwiches, pizzas, sausages on sticks, jelly, biscuits, buns, crisps, peanuts and ... and ... still no smell at all.

What's the point of food that doesn't pong? Weird...

JACK SPLAT

Time to investigate! I landed on a plate and plunged my long proboscis towards an oozy cream cheese sandwich.

Here I come!

But all I got was the terrible taste of plastic. It was the same with a sausage roll and the pizza.

It was as if the food had been covered up with some sort of clingy plastic window!

"How am I going to break through?" I groaned.

I watched from the ceiling as Bogeyboy and the Mouldymeat Kid slouched over to the table.

"When can we eat tea?" asked Mouldymeat. "I'm starving!"

"Mum says we've got to wait," moaned Bogeyboy. "She put cling film on everything to keep our 'grubby little fingers' out."

Mouldymeat grinned. "Cling film can't stop me!" Then he put on a funny deep voice. "I AM SUPER-ANGRY, SUPER-STRONG AND SUPER-HUNGRY, TOO! I CAN RIP THROUGH CLING FILM IN ONE SECOND FLAT!"

With that, he tore off the plastic stuff from a giant bowl of jelly and stuck his big sausagey hand inside.

JACK SPLAT

"Quick," said Bogeyboy, dunking his hand in too. "Don't let Mum see!"

"Good work, boys!" I buzzed over at super-speed. The moment the boys took out their fingers to slurp off the jelly, I flew into the bowl.

"Woo-hoo!" Down I dived on to the wobbly jelly. And ... BOING! Up I bounced again. Up! Down! Up! Down! Up! Down! It was like jumping on a fly trampoline.

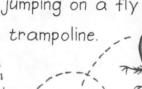

BOING!

JACK SPLAT

"Argh! Stop!" I dug my legs in and clung on. At last I came to a standstill. YUM! The sweet strawberry flavour shot up through my knees and made me wobbly with pleasure.

Jack's super eating!

1 — Land on the jelly.

2 — Vomit up my last meal.

Bubbly bird poo and toilet water

JACK SPLAT

But the jelly was too solid and rubbery for me to slurp up through my proboscis. First I had to puke and wait for my super saliva to dissolve the food.

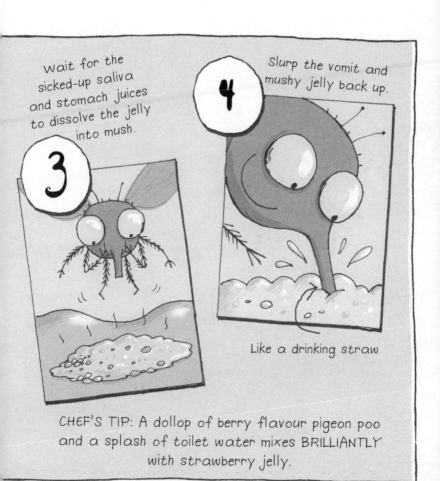

Wait for the sicked-up saliva and stomach juices to dissolve the jelly into mush.

3

Slurp the vomit and mushy jelly back up.

4

Like a drinking straw

CHEF'S TIP: A dollop of berry flavour pigeon poo and a splash of toilet water mixes BRILLIANTLY with strawberry jelly.

JACK SPLAT

I was about to puke again, when Mouldymeat picked up the jelly and shook it.

Wham! Bam! Splat! Ouch!

I lurched sideways and hit my head on the side of the glass bowl.

"Cool! There's a fly. Look!" said Mouldymeat, shaking the bowl so hard I thought my eyes might pop out.

JACK SPLAT

"Watch what you're doing!" I called.

"Put the cling film back!" Bogeyboy laughed. "Let's trap it in there! My mum will FREAK OUT!"

At first, I wasn't bothered. So they'd shut me in with the lovely jelly. Big deal! And at least they'd stopped shaking the bowl about. But it didn't take long before I realized something was wrong... I couldn't breathe!

I waved my bum about desperately, trying to get air through the breathing holes in the side of my body. But there wasn't any air to be had. I felt faint. *There has to be a way to get out of here*, I thought frantically. *I'm an explorer. I have places to go! New food to find! I'm too young to die...*

JACK SPLAT

I flew blearily to the top of the bowl and BOING! hit the clingy ceiling above me. Down I went. Then BOING! Up I bounced from the jelly again. BOING! BOING! BOING! I had to do something... In mid bounce, I threw in a super move, flipped on to my back and stuck my gluey feet to the invisible lid. At last, I stopped bouncing. I hung upside down above the jelly, desperate for breath.

Just then, Mrs Flappy-Arms appeared. "Tea-time!" she called, as she started to rip the cling film off the food. I'd never thought I'd be glad to see her!

"Hey, over here!" I watched as she tore the plastic off the sandwiches, pizzas and sausages on sticks, but as she reached my jelly she stopped.

JACK SPLAT

"Nooo! What about me," I panted. "Let me out!"

Mrs Flappy-Arms took no notice. "No pushing, boys," she said, as she handed out the food.

I pressed up against the glass, looking out at the birthday tea.

Suppose I died in here. Worse still, suppose the ants finally showed up and scoffed the lot!

"Help!" I cried, as my breathless buzzing echoed round the bowl.

Chapter Six
Jelly Food Fun

"Somebody, anybody, save me!" I gasped.

I looked through the glass as the greedy gang of party guests scoffed and slurped and sucked and swallowed ALL the gorgeous gooey birthday tea. "Leave some for me..." I whimpered.

Just when I thought I'd taken my last breath, Mrs Flappy-Arms loomed over my bowl and ripped off the plastic. "Right, boys," she said. "Who wants pudding?"

PHEEEEEEEEEEEEW! Fresh air whooshed through my breathing holes like a dog fart in the wind. YES! I was alive! I flew giddily up out of the bowl ... and straight into Mrs Flappy-Arms's eye.

"Argh!" she cried, flinging her arms in the air and knocking the bowl off the table. The jelly landed PLOP on the floor.

"Wicked!" spluttered Mouldymeat.

"Awesome!" roared Bogeyboy.

"JELLY FIGHT!" cried all the boys at once.

Even though I was still dizzy, my super senses kicked in, and I dodged well out of the way of their grabbing fingers, as they scooped up the jelly.

"Stop, boys!" Mrs Flappy-Arms cried. "STOP THIS INSTANT!"

No one was listening.

"Ants, RETREAT!" ordered the Lieuten-ANT, who'd marched through the doorway at last.

PATHETIC! You wouldn't catch me running away. This was FLY-TASTIC fun!

As globs of jelly flew across the room, I chased after them ... spun over them ... dived under them...

"Outside while I tidy up!" shouted Mrs Flappy-Arms, opening the door and shooing the boys into the back garden. "Right now! Or there won't be any cake."

Moments later, she was back with her stinky-lemon spray. I'd defeated a window, battled a bowl of jelly ... but there was no way I was staying around for that. Making a swift retreat, I flew up to the ceiling.

"Typical!" said a sad voice from the corner. "Parties always get out of hand."

I looked behind me (not by turning round, of course – just by swivelling my eyes).

The voice had come from what seemed to be a ball of dust caught in an old spider's web.

"Fusty?" I said. "Is that you?"

"Yes, it's me." The ball of dust sighed. "I'm just, you know, hanging about."

Fusty is a distant cousin of mine. (That's the thing about us flies, we have a LOT of relations.) My wings drooped. Of all the seven million cousins I could have flown into, why did it have to be Fusty? He is the most miserable insect I know. Nothing EVER seems to make him happy. Not even when we were maggots and found a litre of lumpy, sour milk – not even *that* gave him a buzz.

Now here he was, stuck in a spider's web. To be fair, it didn't look as if he had much to be cheerful about.

"Don't worry!" I said. "I'll think of a super-cunning plan to get you out."

"I wouldn't bother," said Fusty. "You might as well leave me here to die."

"But there's going to be **CAKE** soon!" I said. "I'll bring you a bit, if I can."

"Oh," droned Fusty. "Do you mean that cake there?" (See what I'm getting at? He's the type of fly that doesn't even say **CAKE** in an excited way.)

But he was right. There was my beautiful chocolate **CAKE**. As Mrs Flappy-Arms carried it into the lounge, it seemed to shimmer and sparkle and glow.

Bogeyboy and his friends thundered back in from the garden. They gathered around the **CAKE** and the boys started to sing.

JACK SPLAT

Happy Birthday to you,
Squashed tomatoes and stew,
You look like a monkey,
And you smell like one too!

Was there going to be **CAKE** and squashed tomatoes? This was too good to be true! Best of all, the ants were still hiding behind the door after the jelly fight. Probably scared they'd get trodden on. Weedy little pinheads!

All the more **CAKE** for me!

"Wish me luck, Fusty," I cried. "I'm going in!"

Chapter Seven
Sugar Rush!

The birthday **CAKE** shimmered beneath me. My wings beat faster and faster. My eyes locked on the perfect landing spot ... right in the middle of the chocolate icing.

But as I flew closer there was a strange smell of smoke and melting wax. The air grew hot around me.

"Careful," called Fusty. "That cake looks dangerous!"

JACK SPLAT

"Don't be ridiculous!" I snorted. Typical Fusty. He's too scared to do anything ... so he hides in the corner and ends up caught in a spider's web. Duh!

"There's nothing dangerous about a **CAKE**!" I cried, swooping down. My legs were outstretched, ready to land...

OWWWWWWWW!

OK, so there *was* something dangerous about this **CAKE**! Eight dangerous things to be precise. The reason the **CAKE** was glowing was because Mrs Flappy-Arms had put lighted candles on top.

Was the woman mad? Who'd set fire to a **CAKE**?

Crackle! Sizzle! OWWWWWW!

My left wing-tip was singed in the flames. I flew round in circles, smoke billowing behind me.

I might have had to fly round in circles for ever if I hadn't flown too low and burned the right wing, too.

Crackle! Sizzle! OWWWWWW!

At least that meant I could fly straight again.

I shot up to the ceiling, with smoke trailing from my wings.

"You look like a fire-fly!" Fusty chuckled.

Great! The most miserable fly in the world chooses this moment to turn into Mr Funny!

"Just you wait!"
I smouldered (literally).
"I'm going to have some of
that **CAKE** if it's the last thing I do!"

"It might well be the last thing you
do." Fusty giggled.

"Yeah! Well, you just hang around
and watch," I said, swooping towards
the **CAKE** again. "I'll dodge those
flames, no problem."

JACK SPLAT

I would have too, if Bogeyboy
hadn't blown out the candles in one big
WHOOSH!

"HELLLLLLLLLLLLLLP!" I was thrown
across the room on a mixture of hot
wax and spit.

Only my super flying skills stopped
me ending up SPLAT on the wall.
I looped-the-loop and was back
hovering above the CAKE, quicker than
snot from a sneeze.

VROOOOOOOOOOOOOM!

I dived again, feet
outstretched.

JACK SPLAT

SKID! PLOP! It was a perfect
landing – right in the middle.

I sunk up to my hairy knees in
chocolatey icing and plunged my
proboscis deep into the squishy sponge
below. Oh, Mama! That **CAKE** was
worth the wait. It tasted better
than in my wildest dreams.
(Even the really brilliant dream
where I find a rotten fish head
                    and eat the
          eyeballs all by myself.)

JACK SPLAT

I have to tell you, Buddy-Two-Legs, you miss out on a lot in life by not being a fly. Flies' feet are 10 million times more sensitive to sugar than the human tongue. That means everything we taste is 10 million times sweeter than it would be for you! What I want to know is why wasn't I part of the experiment to prove that? Maybe if I had been, I'd have grown up to be a famous scientist like Sir Flysaac Newton.

SIR FLYSAAC NEWTON

Famous fly scientist who discovered gravity. Now flies know to cling on tight when we walk on the ceiling. Before that we used to just fall down *SPLAT*.

JACK SPLAT

Anyway, the point is, when you humans taste a really delicious slice of chocolate **CAKE**, you go, "Wow!" But, if a fly lands on the same **CAKE**, it's gonna be...

But the sugar-buzz did not last long. By the time I'd puked, Mrs Flappy-Arms was back.

"Time to cut the cake, boys." She stepped forward holding a shiny steel knife – and that was when she spotted me. "Uuuuugh!" she cried. "It's that disgusting fly again! I'll kill it this time!"

JACK SPLAT

"Things don't look good," warned Fusty from his web.

Plip! Mrs Flappy-Arms flipped me on to the tip of the knife and scooped me off the **CAKE** with a flick of her wrist. It was a miracle I wasn't cut in half!

"Squish it!" cried Bogeyboy.

"Splat it!" cried Mouldymeat.

"Stick it to the wall!" cried Spiderboy.

Great! Now everybody had an idea of how to finish me off.

"Don't worry, boys," said Mrs Flappy-Arms. "That revolting little pest has had it this time!"

But, luckily, as she raised her arm, I slid off the edge of the knife and landed on a pile of birthday presents below.

JACK SPLAT

"Come on! Come on!"
I cried, desperately
flapping my wings. But
it was no use. My legs
were stuck to the
wrapping paper by a
blob of icing.

Mrs Flappy-Arms grabbed the nearest
thing to her.

"Not my Lightsaber!" Bogeyboy
moaned, as Mrs Flappy-Arms aimed the
shining blue sword straight at my
head!

This is it, I thought, as my life
flashed before me at supersonic speed.

(If you want to see what that's
like, flick through this book really fast
looking at the pictures and shouting,
"Ahhhhhhhhhhhhhhh! I'm going to die!")

But, like a Jedi fly, I have hidden force within me. With one last mighty pull, I freed my feet from the glob of icing.

ZOOOOM!

I swerved sideways, dodged the Lightsaber and was gone.

Up and up I flew towards the ceiling.

I was alive! I was free! I was...

I was not going to stop!

I was hurtling towards something in the corner ... something dusty and stringy and grey.

SPLAT! I landed feet-first in the spider's web – right beside Fusty's bum.

"Oh dear," said Fusty. "I don't think you wanted to do that!"

Chapter Eight
A Crumbly Ending!

I was well and truly stuck. Yes, me, the great explorer! The more I wriggled, the more the spider's web tightened around me.

There was no escape. I'd be forced to hang out with Fusty for the rest of my life.

Still, I was determined not to become as miserable as him.

"Look on the bright side," I said. "This is an old web. There's no sign of the spider anywhere."

"It'll be back," said Fusty. "Then it'll

suck out our guts like a bee drinking honey from a flower."

"Thanks for that, Fusty!"

Was this really it? Was this how my BIG adventure would end? No **CAKE**. No fame. Just me and Fusty and the jaws of a hungry spider!

That was not a happy thought. Worse still, I then had to watch all the greedy guests take fat slices of my beloved **CAKE** home in their party bags.

JACK SPLAT

Next, the pesky ants arrived to gorge themselves on crumbs.

The fly is trapped. Oh, what bad luck!
He's in the web, and he looks stuck!
But every minus has a plus
Because this means more cake for us!

"Buzz off!" I called, as they marched under the sofa, each carrying a crumb twice their size. There was no way I could just hang around and watch the ants pinch my **CAKE**. I had to think of a way to get me and Fusty out of here before they stole the lot.

But, before long, there was no sign there'd ever even been

a party. Mrs Flappy-Arms
threw paper plates in bin bags,
squirted the table with her mean-clean
spray and shook out the cushions. Then
she got out the vacuum cleaner.

VROOM! Ten swishes of the nozzle
and there wasn't a crumb left!

"If I ever do escape," I shouted, "I'm
going to poop in your cornflakes every
morning!"

"I wouldn't be so noisy, if I were
you," said Fusty. "You might attract
the sp... sp... sp..."

"The what?" I said. "Sp... sp...
spit it out, Fusty!"

"Sp..." said Fusty, waving his
one free leg in the air. He
looked pale – really pale.
Even for him.

"What is it?" I said, suddenly feeling a little nervous.

I looked round and came face to face with six goggly eyes, eight hairy legs and an evil grin! ARGH! The most enormous sp… sp… SPIDER I had ever seen swung backwards and forwards in front of me on a silky thread.

"Yum! Two flies for the price of one," said the spider, swinging closer. "Time for tea!"

JACK SPLAT

She grinned, a trickle of poison dripping from each of her fangs.

"T... t... tea-time?" I stuttered. "If you're hungry, you should try the **CAKE**. It's delicious. The ants took some crumbs under the sofa. I'm sure they'll share."

"Crumbs are for mice," sneered the spider. "I eat *meat*!"

"Yes," I babbled. "But—"

"SILENCE!" she cried. "I do not expect to have to talk to my food!"

She clapped two of her eight legs in the air. "I was going to eat your shrivelled-up friend first..."

Fusty gulped.

"...But you look much more juicy."
She prodded a long, hairy leg into my
tummy.

YIKES! She was so close, I could
smell her rotten breath. She opened her
mouth wide and was about to sink her
poisonous fangs into my head when...

Suddenly, she flew backwards.

"A spider with wings!" groaned
Fusty. "That's all we need!"

But it wasn't wings that were
making her fly.

Mrs Flappy-Arms was now waving
the hose of her vacuum cleaner at the
ceiling. The spider spiralled down, down,
down towards the black mouth of the
tube. But, just as she was about to
be sucked in, she shot up a string of

thread and swung sideways out of the stream of air.

"I'll be back!" she cried, as she landed on Mrs Flappy-Arms's head and scuttled down the back of her neck.

Mrs Flappy-Arms didn't notice. She pointed the vacuum hose in our direction...

WHOOOOOOOOSH! The web shook and we were sucked backwards, spinning helplessly through the air...

ARRRRRRRRGGGGGHHH!

Then everything went dark. Very dark.

And quiet.

"So this is it?" came Fusty's voice out of the gloom. "I'd hoped death might be a bit more exciting."

"No, Fusty!" I cried. "Don't you see?"

"I don't see anything," he moaned. "It's too dark."

"We're not dead!" I laughed, stretching my legs. "We're free! We've been vacuumed!"

"That was pretty lucky, I suppose," said Fusty.

"PRETTY LUCKY? PRETTY LUCKY?" I thundered. "We were about to be slurped to death by a spider! We are TOTALLY the luckiest flies that have

ever lived. We are like the Lucky McFly
cousins of McLuckshire. If luck were
legs, we'd be millipedes by now!"

"Eh?" said Fusty.

OK, I admit, the whole millipede
image was going a bit far, but we had
just had a super-lucky escape from
death. And it was about to get even
better!

"Fusty!" I said, my antennae
bristling. "Can you smell what I smell?"

JACK SPLAT

"Dust?" said Fusty.

"Of course you can smell dust," I groaned. "We're inside a vacuum cleaner! What else can you smell?"

"Crumbs?" said Fusty.

"Exactly!" I cried. "Mrs Flappy-Arms just hoovered the floor. This vacuum is FULL of fluff-covered, fly-sized crumbs of TOTALLY delicious **CAKE!**"

At last, I could have my **CAKE** and

eat it! I rubbed my front legs together, then dipped my proboscis into the biggest, chocolatiest, fluff-and-jelly-coated crumb I could find.

"OOOOOOMMMMMMMMMM! This **CAKE** is truly FLY-TASTIC, Fusty," I spluttered.

We puked and picnicked, gulped and guzzled, slurped and scoffed till our bellies were fit to burst.

JACK SPLAT

"I feel sick," said Fusty.

"Throw up and eat some more."
I grinned.

As I guzzled **CAKE**, nothing could
spoil my mood. Not even Fusty. Not
even the sound of the bossy Lieuten-
ANT and his ant army marching
towards us through the darkness
of the vacuum cleaner.

We smell cake, so we have come
To join you flies and have some fun.

"Welcome, Lieuten-ANT," I cried.
"There's plenty to go round."

I looked up and peered into the
deep darkness of the vacuum cleaner.
I felt like a time traveller lost in
space. Mum would be proud, if she

knew I was out here. I — Jack Splat —
was like the most famous fly explorer
of them all — the Timelord, Dr Poo!

The Timelord, Dr Poo

Featuring the new doctor –
Jack Splat! .

Marvel as he travels
through time and space
armed only with his
sonic poo-driver!
"No need for a Tardis!
I've got wings!"

"What I want to know," said Fusty,
as we finished off the last of the
crumbs, "is how we're going to get out
of here?"

Trust him to put a damper on
things!

"Easy," I said. "I've got a clever
plan. We can just, erm, just—"

JACK SPLAT

Before I could say another word, the ants began to sing.

The only way that you'll get free
Is through the nozzle, don't you see?
We bet the fly pretends he knows,
But he won't think about the hose!

"Hose?" I said. "What about the hose?"

The ants marched past us, down the vacuum hose towards a tiny glimmer of daylight at the end.

Of course! If we'd got in through the hose, we'd probably be able to get out that way too!

"I knew we could get out down there," I called after them. "I was planning to escape through the hose all along."

JACK SPLAT

"Liar," said a squeaky little voice.

"Come on, Fusty," I said, ignoring the tiny ant. "Let's go!"

I flew down the hose, swooping low over the ants.

I was a true explorer now! I could get us all out of here in no time.

"Follow me, pinheads!" I called. "I, Jack Splat, will lead you to safety."

As I flew into the light I did a triumphant loop-the-loop.

"Careful!" said Fusty.

"Don't be such a fuss-pot!" I cried, as I zipped across the lounge at top speed. "Nothing can stop me now! I'm Jack Spla—"

WHAM!
OUCH!

OK, nothing except a window could stop me now.

Fusty giggled.

"Just checking my reflection," I said, as I slid down the glass.

My antennae were bent, I was covered in fluff and my wings were singed. But I still looked handsome, in a tough explorer kind of way.

"I've got to tell you, Fusty," I called, "I'm looking good! I'm Jack Splat – and I'm ready for my next fly-tastic adventure!"

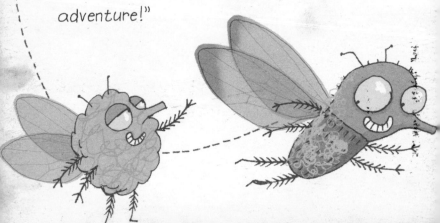